Acknowledgments

Special thanks to Apostle Darryl Winston, Jennifer Lyons,
and Ryan Bolton for the blessing of their special gifts.

Library of Congress Cataloging-in-Publication Data

Watkins, Angela Farris.
Uncle Martin's big heart / by Angela Farris Watkins ; illustrated by Eric Velasquez.
p. cm.
ISBN 978-0-8109-8975-7
1. King, Martin Luther, Jr., 1929–1968—Juvenile literature. 2. African Americans—Biography—Juvenile
literature. 3. Civil rights workers—United States—Biography—Juvenile literature. 4. Baptists—United
States—Clergy—Biography—Juvenile literature. 5. African Americans—Civil rights—History—20th century—
Juvenile literature. I. Title.
E185.97.K5W328 2010
323.092—dc22
[B]
2009052198

Text copyright © 2010 Angela Farris Watkins, PhD
Illustrations copyright © 2010 Eric Velasquez
Photograph on back cover and dedication page copyright © Benedict J. Fernandez
Book design by Maria T. Middleton

Printed and bound in China
10 9 8 7 6 5 4 3 2

Abrams Books for Young Readers are available at special discounts when purchased in quantity for
premiums and promotions as well as fundraising or educational use. Special editions can also be created to
specification. For details, contact specialmarkets@abramsbooks.com or the address below.

ABRAMS
THE ART OF BOOKS SINCE 1949

115 West 18th Street
New York, NY 10011
www.abramsbooks.com

To my daughter, Farris Christine;

my parents, Isaac and Christine (King) Farris;

my brother, Isaac Jr.; my King family cousins;

and especially my grandparents, Martin Luther King Sr.

and Alberta Williams King, whose love inspires generations

—A. F. W.

To the lasting memory of Dr. Martin Luther King Jr.

—E. V.

Have you heard of the man who spoke out, "I have a dream!"?
He was a great civil rights leader and an American hero.
Do you remember his name? I'll give you a hint. His first name
was Martin.

Yes. His name was the Reverend Dr. Martin Luther King Jr.
But to me, it was Uncle Martin. Actually, it was Uncle M.L.

M.L. was our family's nickname for him. The *M* stood for "Martin," and the *L* stood for "Luther." My brother, Isaac; my cousins, Alveda, Alfred, Derek, Darlene, and Vernon; and I all called him Uncle M.L. I liked the sound of his nickname. It was fun to say.

Most people did not know that Martin Luther King Jr. had a family nickname, so usually, when we went out in public, we called him Uncle Martin.

People didn't see Uncle M.L. the way that I saw him. What the world remembers about Martin Luther King Jr. is that he was a man who changed things. They remember that he worked hard to change laws in America so that all people had equal rights.

They remember that he marched and protested and that he made hundreds of speeches and wrote several books. What they saw was a man who inspired thousands of people to join him in helping to change America, but I saw something different. There was something very special about Uncle M.L.

I remember that my uncle loved to spend time with his family and send telegrams while he was away. He loved to laugh and make others laugh.

He loved to work. He loved God
and all people. And something else—
he spoke with a great big voice!

Uncle M.L. worked very long and hard protesting, writing, and speaking, but he spent as much of his time as he could with his wife, my aunt Coretta, and their four children, my cousins Yolanda, Martin III, Dexter, and Bernice. He loved them all very dearly. It was rather amazing that Uncle M.L. still found time to spend with the rest of us!

Uncle M.L. often came to our house for a visit. One time when he came over, I told him how my mother had scolded me. I imitated her voice and pointed my finger as I told Uncle M.L. what she said: "*You broke my pocketbook!*" Although I wasn't trying to make him smile, Uncle M.L.'s smile made me forget how scared I was that I broke my mother's purse. He wanted me to say it over and over again. He thought it was funny.

No matter how hard Uncle M.L. worked or how tired he was, he would still come for a visit. Once he was so tired, he fell asleep on our living room couch—*with his shoes on*! Can you imagine? My mother said we should never lie on the living room couch, and certainly not with shoes on! How could this be?

Uncle M.L. had on his white shirt, his tie, his gold watch, and his black *shoes*! I guess my mother knew how tired Uncle M.L. was from all the good work he was doing and she didn't want to bother him.

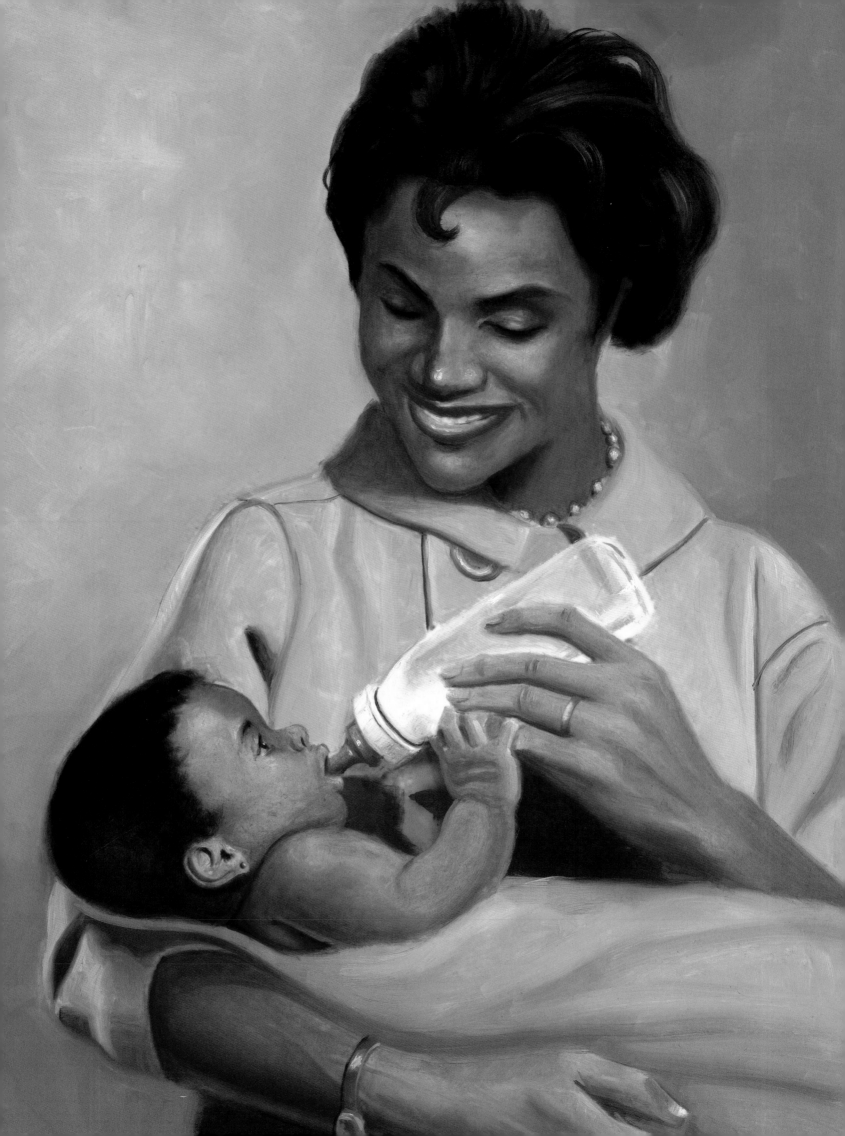

Uncle M.L. stayed in touch with us even while he was out of town. The day after I was born, Uncle M.L. sent a telegram to my mother, his sister Christine, congratulating her on my birth. Uncle M.L. sent it all the way from California to Atlanta, Georgia, where I was born. He was in California working, but still he took the time to welcome me into this world. The telegram said:

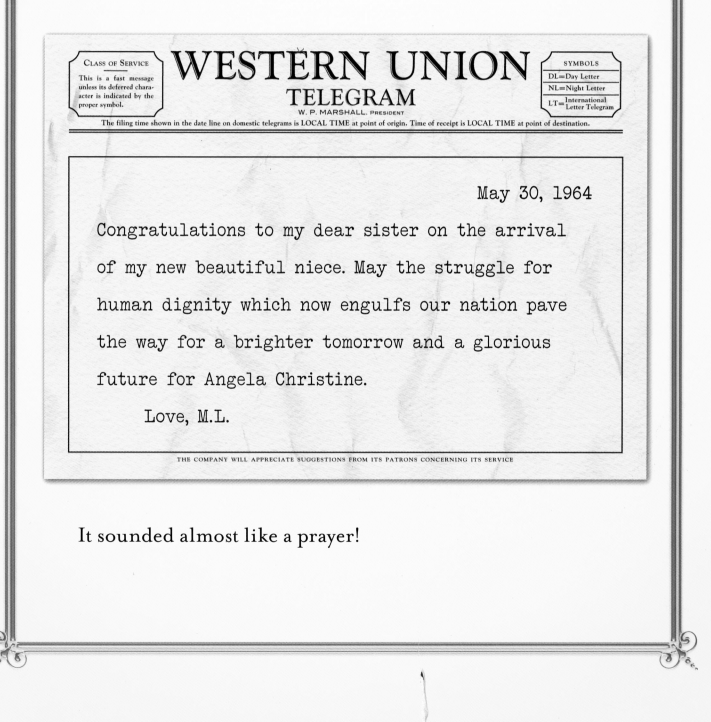

May 30, 1964

Congratulations to my dear sister on the arrival of my new beautiful niece. May the struggle for human dignity which now engulfs our nation pave the way for a brighter tomorrow and a glorious future for Angela Christine.

Love, M.L.

THE COMPANY WILL APPRECIATE SUGGESTIONS FROM ITS PATRONS CONCERNING ITS SERVICE

It sounded almost like a prayer!

Uncle M.L. was a preacher, and a good one, too. He was also co-pastor of our church, Ebenezer Baptist Church in Atlanta, for many years. His father, the Reverend Dr. Martin Luther King Sr. (my granddaddy), was the pastor.

Uncle M.L. loved God, and he loved to preach. He helped people to understand God's love. He wrote many sermons, and he preached to the members of our church about the same thing that he spoke to American citizens about: how to love one another.

Uncle M.L. spoke to thousands and thousands of people during his lifetime. Many people say that he was a great orator, a great speaker. I think it's because Uncle M.L. had such a great voice. It made people pay attention to what he said, and it made them feel good, the same way it made me feel.

Most of the time Uncle M.L. had a serious expression, especially when he was speaking, like when he delivered his "I have a dream" speech. He spoke about the dream of a better America, where all people would love one another, no matter the color of their skin. Laughter was not usually what the world saw when they looked at Martin Luther King Jr.

When he was around us, however, Uncle M.L. laughed a lot. His laughter showed in his face more than in his voice. When Uncle M.L. laughed, his face would light up so that others around him would laugh. Every time I think about it, it makes *me* want to laugh.

Church was where I spent my most favorite time with Uncle M.L.
He and I frequently shared a very special moment, right after church
at Ebenezer. I would stay in the children's nursery during the church
service. When church ended, an adult from the nursery would bring
me upstairs into the sanctuary. Uncle M.L. would stand in front of
the pulpit after his sermon and greet the members of the church who
waited, in a line, to speak to him.

When Uncle M.L. saw me coming, he would step aside from the line, move into the aisle, and bend down. I would run down the aisle in my very best church dress, and with my pigtails flying in the air, to meet him. Uncle M.L. would pick me up and give me a kiss and a great big hug!

In those special moments, I could feel Uncle M.L. saying, *"I love you."*

That's what made Uncle M.L. so special. He had a very, very big heart, and it was all full of love!

Uncle M.L. loved America. He wanted it to be the best country, a country where people of all races and colors would be treated with respect. He worked hard to show people how to change things by using love instead of hate.

Today, people all over the world know about Martin Luther King Jr. They read about him in books. They listen to his speeches, and they read the books that he wrote.

Millions of people visit Atlanta to see where he was born, the church where he preached, and the place where he is buried. There are many streets, schools, and other buildings named in his honor throughout America. Every year, the country celebrates Martin Luther King Jr. Day on the third Monday of January.

It's all because he was an ordinary man with extraordinary love!